NATASHA WING'S
The Night Before
the Dentist

Grosset & Dunlap

In memory of my dentist Jon Swanbom, DDS—NW

To Rosie, who has the biggest, brightest smile in the state—AW

GROSSET & DUNLAP
An Imprint of Penguin Random House LLC, New York

Text copyright © 2021 by Natasha Wing. Illustrations copyright © 2021 by Penguin Random House LLC.
All rights reserved. Published by Grosset & Dunlap, an imprint of Penguin Random House LLC, New York.
GROSSET & DUNLAP is a registered trademark of Penguin Random House LLC. Manufactured in China.

Visit us online at www.penguinrandomhouse.com.

Library of Congress Cataloging-in-Publication Data is available upon request.

ISBN 9780593095690

Special Markets ISBN 9780593521403 Not for Resale

10 9 8 7 6 5 4 3 2

This Imagination Library edition is published by Penguin Young Readers, a division of Penguin Random House, exclusively for Dolly Parton's Imagination Library, a not-for-profit program designed to inspire a love of reading and learning, sponsored in part by The Dollywood Foundation. Penguin's trade editions of this work are available wherever books are sold.

NATASHA WING'S
The Night Before
the Dentist

By Natasha Wing

Illustrated by Amy Wummer

Grosset & Dunlap

'Twas the night before my visit
to go check my teeth.
I really like my dentist.
His name's Dr. Keith.

I've lost four of them already.
And two big ones have come in.
Now another's getting loose.
Soon the wiggling will begin.

I brushed and I brushed
a long time that night.
I wanted to be sure
my smile was super bright.

That night I nestled all snug in my bed,
while visions of toothbrushes danced in my head.

At ten the next morning,
it was time to go.
"Buckle up!" Mom said
as she strapped in JoJo.

The nice guy at the desk
checked us right in.
My sister giggled and flashed
a big toothless grin.

"Now that your forms
are filled in and complete,
go around the corner
and please take a seat."

When what to my wondering eyes should appear
but a brand-new playroom with lots of toys and new gear!
The games—how cool! The toys—how fun!
My sister and I shared our favorite one.

Miss Sonis called my name
and greeted us with a smile.
"The dentist will be ready
in just a short while."

Dr. Keith waved me over
to come sit in the chair.
Then he set out his tools
on the counter with care.

He let me shoot water
from his metal squirt gun.
I hit the target—bull's-eye!
It's the best I've ever done!

Then he put on his gloves and paper face mask. "Which flavor of polish do you want?" he asked.

I sampled them all,
from bubblegum to berry.
I picked out one
that tasted like cherry.

He handed me some goggles
to protect my eyes,
then tilted back my chair—
it was the perfect kid size.

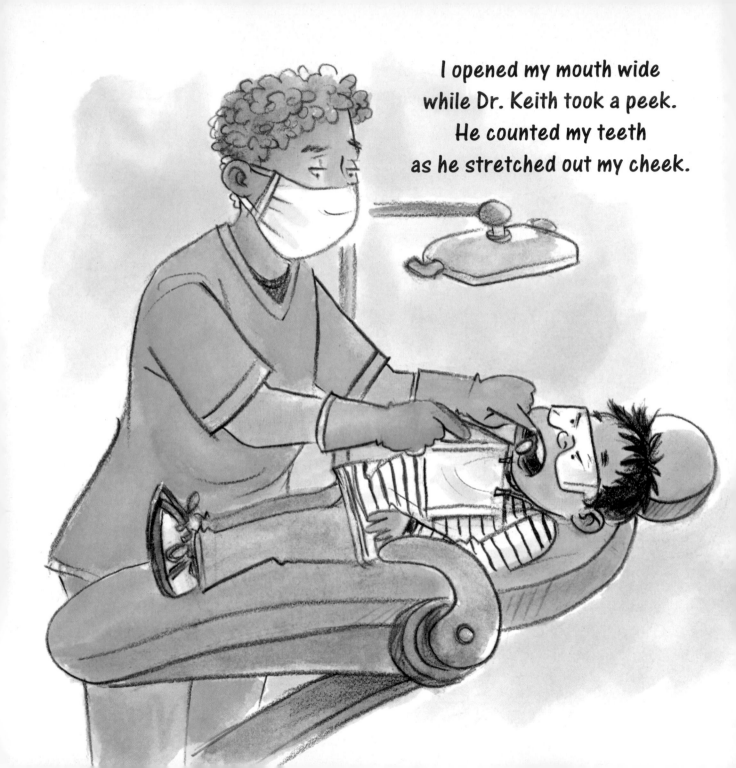

My dentist nodded and said,
"Your teeth look really good!
Try eating less candy
and keep flossing like you should."

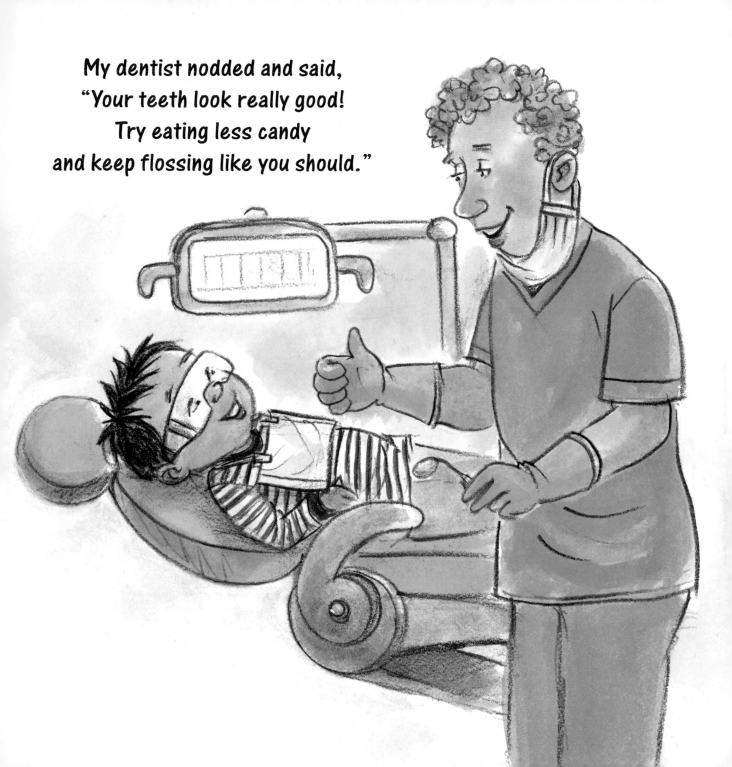

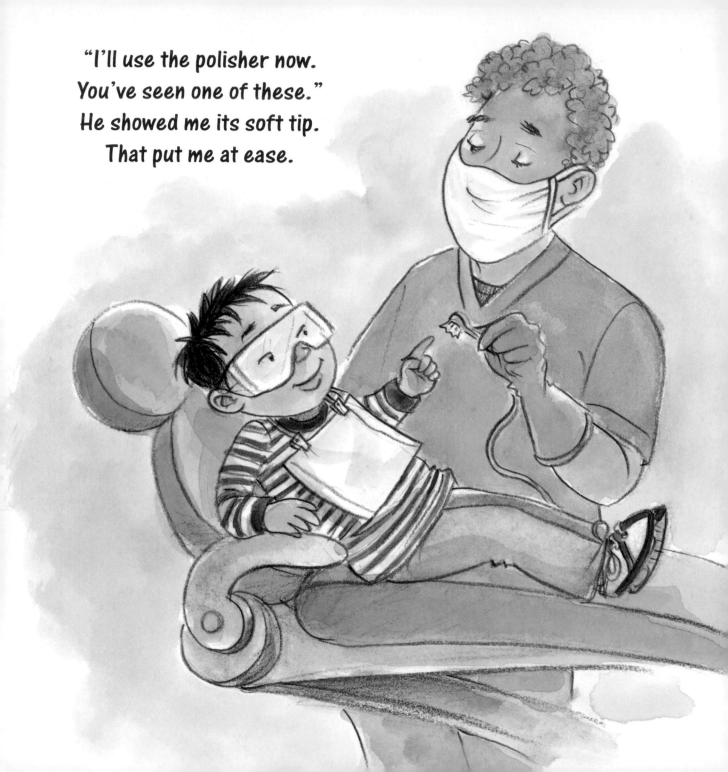

"I'll use the polisher now.
You've seen one of these."
He showed me its soft tip.
That put me at ease.

He turned on the polisher.
"Okay, here it comes!"
I tried not to laugh
'cause it tickled my gums.

He put a straw in my mouth
that sucked up my spit.
"How much longer," I asked,
"do I have to sit?"

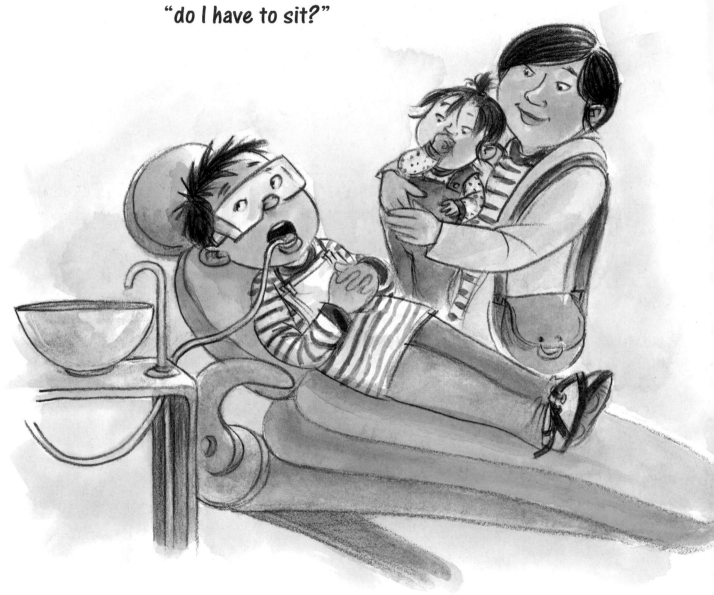

"All done!" said Dr. Keith.
It didn't even hurt!
He gave me a sticker
that I stuck on my shirt.

Then off I went
to get an X-ray.
No cavities at all!
Hip hip hooray!

Miss Sonis gave me a bag
with a tube of toothpaste,
a brand-new toothbrush,
and floss with mint taste.

I got to pick out a prize
from the giant toy chest.
Cool! Chattering teeth!
My dentist is the best.

And oh look—JoJo's first tooth!
It's starting to show.
Soon it will be
her turn to go.